By Day,

By Night

Amy Gibson
Illustrated by Meilo So

BOYDS MILLS PRESS
AN IMPRINT OF HIGHLIGHTS
Honesdale, Pennsylvania

Author's Note

AIDS has left a generation of orphans.
This book is for the millions of children who find themselves alone, whatever the cause.
All of the author's proceeds will be invested in the children of The Global Orphan Project—children who are gifts to the world.

—Amy Gibson

THE GLOBAL ORPHAN PROJECT

Boyds Mills Press
An Imprint of Highlights
815 Church Street
Honesdale, Pennsylvania 18431

Printed in Malaysia
ISBN: 978-1-59078-991-9
Library of Congress Control Number: 2014931585

First edition
Design by Barbara Grzeslo
Production by Margaret Mosomillo
The text of this book is set in Adrianna.
10 9 8 7 6 5 4 3 2 1

For all
who need a hand to hold
—AG

For Lynne
—MS

By day we waken to the sun.

We yawn and stretch, as one by one . . .

We wash.
We brush.
We dress.
We eat.

We greet each other
when we meet.

We buy and sell.

We give and trade.

We offer what our hands have made.

We've work to do and loads to bring,

and tales to tell and songs to sing.

We're carried first

and swaddled tight.

We toddle

till we walk aright.

We all play ball.
We all pretend.

And everybody needs a friend.

We learn to read;

books open doors

to worlds
we've never known before.

We drink the rain

and watch things grow.

We see the seasons

come and go.

We all start small. We all grow old.
We've all been given hands to hold.

We wish. We dream.
We laugh. We cry.
We look. We stop
and wonder why.

When in the west the daylight dies,

by night we sleep beneath the skies.

As one by one we close our eyes,

stars watch and wait, till dawn . . .

We rise.